CINDERELLA

Illustrations by Paige Billin-Frye

APPLESAUCE PRESS

KENNEBUNKPORT, MAINE

D1313872

13-Digit ISBN: 978-1-64643-036-9
10-Digit ISBN: 1-64643-036-0

This book may be ordered by mail from the publisher.
Please include $5.95 for postage and handling.
Please support your local bookseller first!

Books published by Cider Mill Press Book Publishers are available at special discounts for
bulk purchases in the United States by corporations, institutions, and other organizations.
For more information, please contact the publisher.

Applesauce Press is an imprint of
Cider Mill Press Book Publishers
"Where Good Books Are Ready for Press"
PO Box 454
12 Spring Street
Kennebunkport, Maine 04046

Visit us online!
cidermillpress.com

Typography: ITC Caslon 224
Printed in China

1 2 3 4 5 6 7 8 9 0
First Edition

Once there was a man who married a proud and haughty woman. She had two daughters of her own, both as mean spirted as their mother and just as vain.

The man had a young daughter from his first marriage, who was as beautiful as she was kind. The stepmother secretly despised the young girl, but said nothing in front of her husband, as he loved his daughter dearly.

But not long after their wedding, the man became very ill and passed away.

Then, the stepmother showed her true
colors. She became cruel and spiteful, and
forced the young girl to sleep on a straw cot by the
chimney and sit in the ashes and cinders to eat her
meals. Her oldest stepsister called her "Cinderwitch,"
and lorded over her, but the younger stepsister was not
as cruel, and instead called her "Cinderella."

Cinderella was made to do all of the chores around the house: she scoured the dishes, scrubbed the floors, and was in charge of cleaning all of her stepsisters' fine gowns, while she herself was forced to wear rags. But even though her stepsisters had so many beautiful clothes and accessories, Cinderella was still more beautiful than them, for her heart was kind while theirs were full of spite.

It happened one day that the King's son was to give a
ball and invited all persons of high standing to attend. The
stepsisters were both invited, and the girls spent the entire
day choosing what they should wear. Cinderella was made
to iron their dresses and plait their ruffles, and was asked to
judge her stepsisters' outfits, as she had an eye for fashion.

"Why Cinderella," said the younger stepsister, "wouldn't you love to go to the ball?"

Cinderella responded, "Oh, you only tease me, for I am not allowed to go."

"Of course not!" the oldest snapped. "Who would want to see an ugly Cinderwitch at a ball?" But despite their meanness, Cinderella made sure they looked their best, for she was always kind.

When the time arrived for the stepsisters to go to the ball, Cinderella watched them from the window as long as she could, and then ran to her corner by the chimney and started to cry. As she was crying, a spark shot out of the fireplace and exploded into magical light, and a fairy stood in front of her.

"My dear, why are you crying?" the fairy asked.

Cinderella said meekly, "I wish I could go to the ball.
But please, ma'am, who are you?"

"Why, I am your fairy godmother," the fairy said,
twirling in the air. "Come, we must hurry if you are to get to
the ball on time! But first, we must find a large pumpkin."

Cinderella and her fairy godmother found the perfect pumpkin in the garden. Cinderella had no idea how a pumpkin could bring her to the ball, but just as she went to ask, her fairy godmother tapped the pumpkin with her wand and it turned into a beautiful, gilded carriage. Then she waved her wand and six small lizards and one large mouse ran out from the pumpkin patch. She tapped each gently on the head and they transformed into six footmen and a jolly carriage driver.

The fairy godmother nodded at her handiwork and turned to Cinderella. "Now, we cannot have you attend the ball in those rags!"

With a swirl of her wand, Cinderella's rags transformed into a beautiful gown. The fairy godmother gave Cinderella a pair of glass slippers and a grave warning.

"Remember, dear, my magic will only work until midnight.
After that, everything will return as it was." Cinderella promised
she would leave the ball on time and set off for the palace.

Every guest at the ball stood in awe as Cinderella entered the ballroom. The violins fell silent and all eyes were drawn to the beautiful newcomer. Even the stepsisters, who did not recognize Cinderella without her cinders and rags, glared in envy.

The King's son escorted her to the most honorable seat and spent the rest of the night dancing with her, where her grace was admired by all.

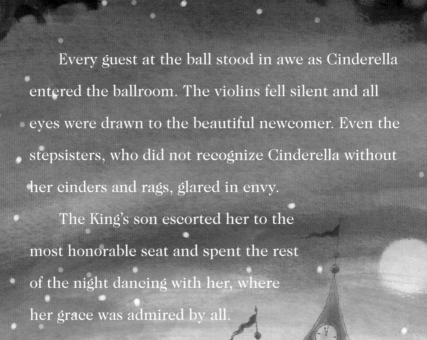

As her last dance finished, Cinderella heard the clock strike the first note of midnight, and she ran in haste from the palace, leaving a single glass slipper behind. Just as she arrived home, her carriage turned back into a pumpkin, her footmen and driver became small animals again, and her beautiful dress became rags. But she still had one glass slipper, which she cherished and hid from her stepsisters.

The next day, the Prince issued a royal decree that every woman in the land should try on the glass slipper, for he had fallen in love with its wearer. When it came time for the slipper to visit the home of Cinderella, her stepsisters fell over each other to have their turn, but they did not fit the slipper. Cinderella, who knew the slipper was hers, asked for her turn, and before her stepmother could argue she slipped on the slipper, which fit perfectly. Her stepmother protested that there must be a mistake, but Cinderella produced the second slipper, and her stepmother fell silent.

Cinderella was taken to the Prince, who found her beautiful even in her rags, and they were married soon after. And Cinderella, who was no less kind than she was beautiful, offered her stepsisters a place to live in the palace, and forgave them for their cruelty, but the Prince forbade her stepmother from ever visiting the palace again.

The End

About Applesauce Press

Good ideas ripen with time. From seed to harvest,
Applesauce Press crafts books with beautiful designs, creative
formats, and kid-friendly information on a variety of fascinating topics.
Like our parent company, Cider Mill Press Book Publishers,
our press bears fruit twice a year, publishing
a new crop of titles each spring and fall.

Write to us at:
PO Box 454
Kennebunkport, ME 04046

Or visit us online at:
cidermillpress.com